Smokie Forever

Best Wishes

Dr. John H Williams

8/04

Smokie Forever

John H. Williams

iUniverse, Inc.
New York Lincoln Shanghai

Smokie Forever

iUniverse, Inc.

For information address:
iUniverse, Inc.
2021 Pine Lake Road, Suite 100
Lincoln, NE 68512
www.iuniverse.com

ISBN: 0-595-29340-9

Printed in the United States of America

Contents

Preface

Hi everybody! My name is Smokie. Sit back and enjoy the story of my life. I'll bet you've never met a cat like me. You see, I'm a Manx from the Isle of Man. Parts of that small island are pretty wild. The climate is mild and that's pretty neat because my relatives could find food and shelter all year long.

I don't look like most cats either. You see I have a big M right in the middle of my forehead. According to legend, it's supposed to have been put there so everyone would know I was from the Isle of Man. That's not the only oddity about my looks. I don't have a tail and my cheeks are so full and rounded they blend right into my short neck. If you look at me sideways, you may think I'm deformed because my front legs are shorter than my hind legs. My hind legs are powerful enough to climb a tree or to kick the tar out of any bully. With such long hind legs, my shoulders arch back to a high, well-rounded rump that makes me sort of swagger when I walk. And that's just fine because it goes with my cocky attitude.

I sure do have a different personality. I like to be in charge and I seldom meow like most cats. But I'll growl like a dog or yell like a mad mountain lion. I'm quiet, but active, shy but friendly, witty but reserved and clever but trusting. I know this sounds like a lot of contradictions, but that's me.

I'll love a whole family, but most of the time I form a close attachment to one *special* person. I love to play games and do many of the things a dog likes to do. I guess that's why I'm sometimes thought of as a dog lover's cat.

If you stop paying attention to me, I may remind you that I'm still here by bumping your leg with my well-rounded, high rump. If that doesn't work, I'll tell you that it's time for me with a soft swat or a little love bite. Read on to learn about my adventurous life.

Chapter 1

My Beginning

My two sisters and I were born in a drafty barn. The barn had a large, open room with beams all across the top and halfway down from the roof. There were rooms filled with bales of hay. Down the hill from the barn was a small log cabin perched on a cliff, which overlooked a sandy beach and a large body of water called the Chesapeake Bay.

A little girl and her brother lived in this cabin with their mother and father. The mother and children loved us, but they couldn't let the father know just how much. The father only let us inside by the wood stove when the weather was very cold. He always complained about how much it cost to feed us. Besides, he didn't even consider us real cats because we didn't have a tail. He said we were always in the way and getting into things. But still, the warmth of the wood stove made me feel cozy, as I snuggled up with my mother and sisters. When I woke up one morning, I found out that the father had given one of my sisters away. With little to eat, and being pushed around, I figured I needed to learn how to survive. Luckily, the father would leave in the morning and wouldn't return until evening. When the children weren't busy with their chores, we would play hide and seek, chase a ball, or play some other game.

One day the children had to go to a place called school. It sure was lonely without them. But it gave our mother time to teach us how a cat should behave. So we had some real fun times, and began learning cat habits from our mother.

Once, after school, the children played with us instead of finishing their chores. When their father got home he was very mad at them and threatened to give us all away. On top of this, I had found some milk in a glass on the table which I started to drink. It was so good, I didn't hear the father coming. Uh, oh, it was his milk! Well, he was already mad at the children, so this was too much. He threw me off the table, opened the door, and kicked me outside. Man, those boots were really hard!

Being so scared, I didn't feel how much pain I had. On top of that, it was cold and now I couldn't get near the stove to get warm. Suddenly, I saw my sister and mother come sailing out the door too. It was a good thing for me though, because my mother kept her senses about her and led us back to the barn. We found a spot behind a bale of hay that shielded us from the cold drafts. Then, with my mother's comforting licks, and with my sister's snuggling, I was able to go to sleep.

Next morning, my mother took my sister and me on a hunting trip through the bushes and around the buildings. We found a few mice and a bird in the bushes. Boy, did my sister and I have a lot to learn in order to be able to catch a meal!

So for many days, our mother did all the hunting. She told us to be alert and to be quiet and still, which was hard for us. We learned how patience was a good habit to learn. She taught us to turn our ears and listen for the tiniest movements. Sometimes, however, the movements turned out to be only brush blowing in the wind. After awhile we learned to sense the difference between possible food and only the wind. For now, at least, the father let the mother and children put some food for us in the barn.

With time passing on into months, it began to get warmer outside and lots of mice, birds, and bugs were hustling about. I got to thinking that, with the weather being good, I should leave home.

When I told my mother about my plan, she tried to talk me out of going. She said it wouldn't be easy because there were dangers out there that I didn't know about. I told her I was sure I could make it and asked her if she would come with me. But my mother couldn't leave my sister who was afraid of the big, dark woods.

So, after lots of advice from my mother, and with my sister begging me to stay, I still decided to leave. I ate the food that was still in our bowl, drank some milk and headed up the hill into the unknown. Full of confidence, I went off to see the world.

Chapter 2

Leaving Home—An Adventure Into the Unknown

The hill was higher than it looked, but my powerful hind legs were great for this kind of climbing. Very soon I came to a hard, black road that was warm from the sun shining on it. This would be a nice place to sleep. But, just as I was thinking about a cat nap, I heard a roaring sound. A big car came around the bend moving very fast. I really had to get off of the road as quickly as I could or it would hit me. This must be one of the dangers my mother had told me about. Putting my hunting skills to use I listened for any more noises like the car had made. Looking both ways, left and right, and seeing and hearing nothing, I ran across to the other side where there was good old dirt, grass and bushes. After that experience with the car, I figured I had better move more carefully. Who knows what else could be out there. So I put my hearing on high alert, kept a watchful eye out for any movement, and started using my nose to notice any unusual smells. I came upon a small path that smelled like it must have been used by a rabbit. Whether I could catch that rabbit or not, it was a sure bet that this path was safe, since rabbits are very cautious and try to stay away from danger. So, I started down the little, matted path through a lot of tall trees and underbrush. Every so often, I would stop and listen just to be sure all was safe.

Suddenly, I came upon two sets of tracks. If these were tire tracks and a person was in the car, maybe I could find some easy food. Then I sensed there was something big lurking in the overgrown bushes of the path, so I decided it would be smart to slink into the unknown woods. Just as it seemed as though the weeds and brush would never end, I saw a car right in front of me. I crouched down quietly and let out a very low warning growl...grrrrr. It didn't move, so I crept closer. That's odd, all of the tires were flat and several of the windows were gone. I stuck my head carefully inside. A high loud squeal and a thumping sound scared me so bad that I banged my head on the door trying to get away. As I stopped beside a brush pile, I realized nothing was chasing me and that the thumping was a rabbit running away from me. I was hoping he didn't know how scared I really was.

I was getting a little hungry, since this was the time the family had brought me something to eat. Had I made a mistake leaving the cabin, my family and the children? Being more sleepy than hungry, I returned to the car, curled up on the soft, cushiony seat and went to asleep. The sound of a soft rain woke me up; but, I wasn't getting wet and the cushion was still warm, so I decided to go back to sleep and wait for it to quit raining. I awoke to see the sun had come up and was peeking right at me through the trees. I jumped out of the car and began moving through the woods away from the sun. I wasn't familiar with these woods, so I figured I had better take notice of everything.

Things were still a little damp, but at least it was warmer than when I was in the barn. I had to find something to eat because I was starved. So I did what my mother had taught me to do. I smelled, looked and listened. Suddenly, I heard a slight movement in the brush. Jumping toward the sound, I caught my first meal as a mighty hunter. I proudly puffed out my thick, furry chest and strutted onward.

My mother had told me that whenever I began to feel too cocky, something would always happen to put me in my place and bring me back to reality. Sure enough, all of a sudden I found myself running from a big dog. It seemed to me that I was doing exactly what the mouse I caught had done. So, I stopped running and took a stance. As the dog rounded a large tree, he was startled to see my back up and to hear me let out a screeching yell. The dog stopped in his tracks. A dog can't possibly let a cat scare him off. So he slowly started towards me, thinking I might change my mind and run. But I roared and growled again, even more fiercely. Now the dog tried the old trick of a lunge straight at me to show he wasn't afraid and that he was much more powerful than me. Just as he lunged at me I leaned back against the tree and, using the tree as my support, I kicked my long, powerful hind legs out and pulled razor sharp claws down the dog's face and nose. With a bleeding nose and face, the dog decided it was better to swallow his pride and leave to go lick his wounds. I knew then I could be brave and that I was a pretty good fighter. I also had learned about another danger.

Just as I was about to explore a hollow log for a possible shelter for the night, I heard a stomping sound. Just a little way ahead, I saw some smaller trees which could provide a safe perch if the stomping meant danger. I scampered toward the trees and spotted one with fairly good sized branches. I used my strong hind legs to shinny up the tree high enough to view the field. Then I saw what was making the stomping noise. It was a large brown deer with a big set of antlers. My mother had told me that deer would not intentionally hurt me but, if the deer were scared, I might be hurt by their pointed hooves. From my perch, I had seen his hooves making the stomping sounds and had gotten a good smell so I could recognize him later. The branch gave way and I fell to the ground. The noise startled the deer. He gave a short snort and ran to another field. It was then I saw a mother deer and her baby running after him. Within seconds all three had crossed the second field and were a safe distance into the woods.

Being curious about what the deer were eating in the first field, I sauntered over only to find some old ears of corn left on the ground. They were all hard, dry and tasteless. Moving across the field, away from the direction the deer had gone, I saw a cabin that was like the one I had left. Maybe there was food to be found over there. I looked to the left and to the right and I smelled and listened but there was nothing. So I darted across the field to a triangle of grass and hid in some bushes in the middle of two roads. From under the bushes I was able to get a better view of the cabin, where I spied a pan and bowl on the steps of a porch. It was food. I was eating so fast I didn't hear something moving around the corner. Looking up I saw a cat that looked almost like me, except he had a tail. I guess this was his home turf and, judging from his looks, he had been in quite a few fights. I was too full to fight or run so I slowly backed away, growling at him just as I had growled at the dog. This made the cat think twice before picking a fight. We began the ritual of allowing each other to back gracefully away, dismissing the need to fight. After that experience, I felt like I needed to hurry up and find a home of my very own.

Just past a bamboo thicket, I followed another dirt road that was so overgrown I knew it hadn't been used recently. The trees and growth, on either side of the road, opened into several gardens. I heard a loud truck in the distance across the gardens. The truck stopped and someone got out. This was worth investigating for a possible home. I was able to see a long building with the truck outside, but no one was in sight. I was hoping there would be something to eat over there and a place to stay for the night.

So, looking in both directions, I moved cautiously across the hard road next to the long building. On this end of the building were some garbage cans with lots of different smells. I climbed onto the wooden frame that held the garbage cans to see what I could find.

Most of the garbage cans had a lid on them, and only one had a lid tilted back. Inside was part of a sandwich with some meat left in it. Needless to say, it tasted just as good as it smelled. I hadn't realized how hungry I was. There also was a partially filled cup of milk. I had to stick my head inside to reach the milk. When I finished it, I found my head was stuck inside the cup. Frantically, I twisted and turned, falling off the wooden frame. As I fell, the cup caught on the frame and was pulled off my head.

I guess I created more noise than I thought because a man came running out of the other end of the building with another man right behind him. One man was bad enough, but two! I flew around back of the building and hid behind a pile of mulch. I knew the men didn't see me because they were looking toward some trees and undergrowth to see if an animal was running away. It seemed that by staying still and very quiet I was able to be safe until they quit looking and went back around front. On their way, they put the lid back on the can, and then went inside.

At the other end of the building was another bamboo thicket. Up a slight hill from the thicket was a house which would be worth investigating. But for now, the bamboo thicket provided a safe haven in which to get some sleep.

As I was trying to relax before dozing off to sleep, I began thinking about my future. I noticed the house was not too far from my hiding place. I wondered if someone lived there and whether *that* could become my home.

When I awoke, it was still dark but I was awfully hungry. I remembered the bin that held the garbage cans, but the lids were all placed back on the cans. Suddenly, I heard the sound of small paws coming out of the woods beyond the house, yet I couldn't see anything. Then under a bright street light, I saw a raccoon. The raccoon went straight to the garbage cans and climbed up on the bin. Using the side of the bin for leverage, he worked his paws like little fingers to pry the lid off the cans. Inspecting each one, he seemed to be having quite a bit of luck finding food. I stood up to stretch. I guess the raccoon heard me because he let out a small whirring chatter and returned to his eating. Evidently for him a cat was nothing to worry about. As I approached he stopped eating, jumped down, and showed his teeth using that same chatter, only louder. He was warning me not to get too close, and I could tell he wasn't afraid of me. I sat down to think about my situation. The raccoon, seeing that I had assumed a sitting position, figured I was no longer a threat. He quickly returned to his eating. When he moved down to the other end of the bin, I took a chance and jumped up on the end of the bin he had left. He looked up, chattered softly, and returned to his eating, sensing that I was not a danger. He ate his fill and hung down from the can, dropping easily to the ground. He went across the road and before long he had disappeared down a dirt road that led into the woods.

After eating, I was happily full again so I jumped down and ventured toward the hill in front of the house. I had heard what sounded like another cat from inside the house; but I had some more exploring to do.

The moon was glowing brightly, allowing me to see clearly in all directions. On top of the hill, I could see the dirt road that the raccoon had taken. Heading left, the road divided and went down two hills. Between the two roads was another big barn. I knew it wasn't the same one where I was born because it looked and smelled slightly different. I was getting kind of sleepy again, so I headed for the barn to see if it had any straw I could use for a bed. I thought that after I got some sleep, I should explore the two roads to look for a nice home of my own.

Chapter 3

A Search Begins for a New Home

When I got to the barn, I poked my head in and saw a large room. On the far side of this room was a flat wagon that had some old burlap on it. Jumping up on the wagon, I found the burlap to be quite comfortable as I kneaded it with my front paws. It was a little rough, but a lot softer than the ground. It was very quiet and soon I was sound asleep.

At daylight, I crawled under the wallboards of the barn away from the house on the hill. Whoooops! I slid over the edge of a hill and tumbled down a few feet until I was able to grab onto a small tree with my claws. Looking down the hill, I could see two houses almost straight across from me. I realized that I didn't know what was in these houses. Besides, I remembered that I had heard another cat in the house on the hill. Using my powerful hind legs, I was soon beside the barn again. At the end of the barn was a wall I could hide behind before I went any farther. On the other side of the wall, I saw a slight slope with grass that ended at the edge of a hard road. Looking to the right, I could to see the house on the hill. If there was a cat in that house, I might be able to make a friend. At the very least, there might be some cat food in the bowls I had seen on the porch.

Suddenly, I heard a car coming up the road behind me. I immediately ran under the doors where I had entered the barn the night before. I had to watch that car to be sure I hadn't been seen. Whew, the car went on around the corner and out of sight. I didn't hear any more cars so, looking both ways, I crossed the road and headed toward the house on the hill.

When I was close enough, I could see a porch that would be a short, easy run to get under. I made a beeline to the porch and found that it went clear around underneath the bowls I had seen. There was even a set of steps leading up to the bowls. I crouched very low and almost slithered up to the porch. I couldn't see anyone through the glass doors that opened into the house, so I boldly walked right up to the bowls. Sure enough there was dried cat food in one bowl and fresh water in another. I couldn't decide whether I was thirstier or hungrier. So I moved from bowl to bowl; first drinking and then eating. Just as I finished the cat food and most of the water, I heard another cat inside. It sounded like a girl cat, so I called to her with one of my mrrowws.

There she was, a beautiful white fluffy furred, little girl. She was so pretty that I forgot the glass door and ran smack into it as I rushed to greet her. Well, I guess that startled her because she let out a howl and sprang at the door, mouth open and claws out. I'm sure glad that the door was closed.

Maybe she was mad because I ate her food, I thought. Then it dawned on me that I must have looked dirty and ragged because she was clean and ladylike, except for that awful temper. Other-wise, I'm sure she would think I was handsome. Then she howled again and charged the door.

Maybe it was time for a quick exit. I flew down the steps and under the porch, just as I heard the door open and close. Someone had come out on the porch. I had to hide! I saw an opening in the wall of the house that looked like one of the cement blocks had been removed. With no time to think matters over, I went through the hole under the house. It was dark and my eyes hadn't become accustomed to the dimness yet. I stayed very still near the hole and its a good thing I did because someone was coming down the steps. It was a woman with a broom in her hand. She looked all around and then started back up the steps. Pausing, she came back down the steps, bent over, and looked under the porch. She must not have been able to see me because she went to the end of the porch and looked under it on the side next to the garden. Being satisfied that there wasn't anything there, the woman went inside and closed the door. That was a close call! I knew I needed to be more careful and always plan a way to escape.

When my eyes adjusted to the dim light, I saw a small room at the other end of the house. The room was nice and warm, with heat coming from a furnace. A short distance across the room was a set of wooden steps. I wanted to know where the steps went, so I climbed slowly up toward two doors that were shut. At the bottom of the doors was a space that wasn't big enough for me to squeeze under, but big enough for me to look under and see the barn where I had spent the night. I figured if those doors were open I'd have a shortcut back to the barn. I pushed with all my might, but the doors were too heavy for me to push up enough to squeeze out. This wore me out. It was warm and I felt safe, so I laid down on some rags and nodded off to sleep.

It was dark when I awoke so I went outside to the bowls on the porch. Luckily there was some food still there. When I finished eating I continued my search for a new home. I remembered the two houses behind the barn and picked the closest house to investigate. It seemed to have all the places a cat would need in which to explore, play, and be comfortable. I wondered if there was a nice family inside.

It was starting to get dark, so I decided to chance going to the house where the pretty cat lived to get some dinner. It seemed that in no time I was at the steps to the porch. I ate and then thought I would just peek inside in case the pretty girl cat wanted to see me. I called lowly. Sure enough, there she came toward the door howling.

She dove at the door with her mouth open, fur bristling, and claws out. Behind her was the woman with the broom. Frantically, I ran down the steps towards the bamboo thicket. I was too scared to sleep and too afraid to try to go back past the house to get to the barn. So, moving farther back through the bamboo thicket, I found a few trees and, beyond the trees, I came out across from the barn. I went quietly into the barn and fell asleep under the wagon. I was so exhausted that I didn't wake up at all until the sun was already up.

Chapter 4

A New Home At Last

It seemed like so long a time since I had been around people, and the ones I did see weren't too friendly. I didn't want to become like a feral (wild) cats because their lives are always full of dangers and they don't have anyone to love them. They don't even know where their next meal is coming from or even if there *is* going to be a meal each day. No, I've just got to find a home, I thought to myself.

I started thinking about the big house I had visited the day before and I went back for a closer look. I thought as I went down the road it had seemed rather nice. I came upon a well-worn path through the woods which I followed until the big house suddenly appeared in front of me.

I saw a doorway and walked over to it very cautiously. I noticed that there was what seemed to be a covered hole in the door. I was able to push the cover open and, putting my head in, I could see a workshop. I climbed inside and walked over to a small door with glass panes, through which I saw a long room. Following my natural curiosity, I spent some time getting familiar with the workshop. Then with a last look around, I headed back to the door. After a few trial and errors, I was able to get back through the covered hole and out of the workshop. I was really worried for fear I wouldn't be able to get back out. I still hadn't seen much of the outside of the house, so I walked up a slight slope until I came to the front yard. I crossed the front yard and found myself on the other side of the house near a porch. Moving down this side I discovered that I had gone all the way around the house. Well, that didn't turn up anything exciting to explore.

But then I noticed a mole hole and thought I had heard a movement. I reached in with my front paws, but I couldn't feel anything. I dug a lot of dirt away and found a tunnel. I kept digging the dirt away from the top of that tunnel. But before I could reach him a mole scurried farther into the tunnel and went farther underground. I didn't feel like digging any more to catch one small mole, instead I headed on around back and came to a set of stairs that led up toward a deck.

It was time to find out about the upstairs of the house so...... up to the deck I went. At the top of the stairs, a container filled with a red liquid caught my eye.

Then I saw two more containers filled with the same red liquid farther down the railing of the deck.

Lo and behold, small hummingbirds started buzzing around these containers. They were so fast, that I finally had a real challenge to see if I could catch one. I was watching the hummingbirds, fascinated by their antics and flying patterns, when I realized that the sun was beginning to go down.

I was so intent watching the hummingbirds that I hadn't payed any attention to the noises inside. Suddenly, I felt worried and started to go back; when I was within a few feet of the steps, I heard the door knob turning. I moved as quickly as I could, crouching low to the deck. Then with a sudden burst of speed, I ran down the steps and into the woods.

When I was a safe distance away from the house, I squatted down and peered back. A man had come onto the deck and was calling, "Here kitty, kitty, kitty." I didn't move. But I wondered if he had seen me and was calling to *me*. Well, it seemed better to be safe than sorry, so I stayed hidden behind a tree stump.

The man went back inside and closed the door, but I kept watching. I'm glad that I had waited, because it wasn't long before the man came back out and put a plate beside a bowl on the deck. Then a woman came out of the house. They both looked toward the woods and, not seeing anything, they went inside.

As I waited, I saw the lights in the house go out and it got quiet. Even though I was still nervous, I smelled something real good, so I ran towards it. Back on the deck, I discovered that the smell was a wonderful, meaty cat food with some dried food on the side of the plate which I quickly devoured. Sticking my nose into the bowl, I tasted warm milk and egg. I was thinking that I could put up with that kind of meal every night.

Uh oh, I heard a noise near the door inside the house. I ran to get away but, halfway down the steps, the door opened. I was so scared that I squeezed between the railings of the steps and jumped down to the ground. Then, oh no, a bright light came on that lit up the entire side yard. The light was so bright that I knew I would be seen if I dashed for the path, so I crouched in the ground cover behind a small tree.

The man came out and the woman was right behind him. "What did you see?" she asked anxiously.

"It looked like a wisp of smoke!," he said. Little did I know that from that moment on these people would call me *Smokie*. Seeing that I had eaten most of the food and drank half of the milk, they took the plate and bowl inside. It was time for me to move to a safer place away from those people. So, I returned to the barn and snuggled down beneath the wagon to sleep for awhile. As I began to doze off, I began thinking about my mother and sister. I wondered how they were or if the man had given her away like he had with my other sister. I really wish they had come with me. I thought together we would have been just fine. Then I fell asleep.

It was still dark when I awoke, and I was in the mood to do some more exploring. I headed toward the road but decided not to push my luck again with that nasty cat and the woman with the broom, since she almost got me on the last visit and was probably watching for me now.

I went the other way until I came to a log cabin. I went under it to a porch on the back. Finding a torn spot in the screen, I was able to get into the porch. I stood on an old chair to look in a window, but nothing seemed interesting and I couldn't find a way to get inside. Going back out, I crossed the road and went down a ravine. Following a path, I spotted the house where I had been fed earlier. Wow, this was neat—I knew another way to get back to this house, if other ways were not safe.

It was starting to get light and I was hungry enough to chance looking on the deck of the big house to see if the people had put more food out. I ran across the deck toward the plate and bowl, pausing only long enough to peer in the door to be sure it was safe. The man and woman were asleep inside and probably wouldn't hear me. Sure enough there was milk and food again.

The weather was mild and the sun was coming up quickly, so I figured I could take a cat nap in the woods near this house and not have to travel so far to get a good meal. I found a low spot filled with leaves. This spot was lower than the yard and beneath two fallen trees, so I was out of sight. The sun warmed the air and the leaves with a few rays filtering onto me through the brush. I was soon asleep, but with all of my senses still on alert.

I heard a door open and I awoke to see the man go down to the shed and return with a bucket filled with bird seed. He was coming up the steps toward me, so I crouched as low as I could. He didn't see me, but went to the bird feeder and filled it with fresh seeds. He began looking carefully at the bushes by the shed and continued up the hill in the woods. He seemed to be looking at every plant as he explored the hill. I thought it would be kind of neat to have a friend who was as curious as me. The man cut through the brush and vines clearing a way back to the center of the yard. Wiping his brow, he walked over by a fountain and sat down on a railroad tie. I was so tempted to go over and see if he was friendly, but I just couldn't overcome my fear. However, the birds didn't seem to be afraid of him. They flew down to eat at the feeder with him still sitting beneath it. I decided to be satisfied just to watch and learn more about him.

The man filled the fountain so the birds had plenty of clean water. I was beginning to get the idea that he took care of the yard, helped make the area cleaner, and fed the birds. If he did all this, I could understand why he would also put food out for me. He went in the workshop door and when he didn't come back out, I had to go see if he was there. I peeked in, but I didn't see him, so I climbed the steps and looked in the glass doors. He caught me staring at him and started to move toward the door. As he came out of the door I ran for the steps. But instead of just calling, "Here kitty, kitty, kitty," I heard him say, "Come here Smokie."

I jumped into the woods by the path and then crouched by the leaf pile. He came to the edge of the deck and looked toward the woods and up the side of the house behind the thicket of bushes. All the while he kept calling the name Smokie.

I didn't think I was quite ready to chance being caught by this man, so I stayed put. He went back in the house and returned with some fresh food. But before he went back inside he called, "here's some more din...din Smokie." I guess din...din meant food. It was getting dark, so I felt safer returning to the deck to eat.

As I started toward the steps, I heard the door open quietly. I darted up the side of the house to hide behind the bushes. The man came to the top of the steps and again called, "Smokie, Smokie, come here boy. It's okay, I won't hurt you." I almost started to go up there, when I saw the woman come out beside him. I heard him tell her that he had gotten a good look at me. He described me to her very well. "He has to be a Manx cat, although it is unusual to find one as a stray. So, I hope he will come back to stay," he said. Then they went back inside.

Lying down, I kept a close eye on the house. After it had been dark for awhile, the bedroom door to the deck opened ever so slightly, and I could hear the man calling, "here Smokie, come on up here boy." I wondered if he meant it. I waited for a short time and then crept up the steps onto the deck. Lo and behold, the door was open slightly. Peering around the corner of the door, I could see the man was lying on a blanket on the floor at the foot of the bed. When I stuck my head in, he didn't move. So, I went farther inside and he still didn't move. But he did say in a whisper, "come on in Smokie. It's okay," he said, still speaking softly. I guess it's now or never I thought to myself. I moved slowly toward him and he stretched his hand out and laid it on the floor. I approached his hand, ready to run in an instant. Moving his hand back and forth, he made motions like he was petting me. All the while he softly repeated the name......"Smokie." Now I couldn't resist. I moved under the hand and it continued to gently pet me. It felt good. I moved closer and, lying on the blanket, my head touched his fore-head. When he didn't move, I felt safe enough to fall asleep.

I awoke with a startled feeling before I remembered how I had gone to sleep with this man. He awoke and left the room but I stayed snuggled on the soft blanket. He returned, slowly going past me to close the door. For some reason, I didn't feel trapped, and was sure that he would let me go out if I wanted to. He spoke softly to me, petted me one more time, and climbed into bed. I put my head back down and dozed off contentedly. I was sure that I had at last found my new home.

I realized that my attention needed to turn toward training these people about how I expected to be treated. I was sure this would take time, but knew that I could do it with a little work. I remember wondering if they were aware of how strongly they would accept me as part of their family. In the meanwhile, I figured I had better get plenty of sleep in order to begin training them the next day.

Chapter 5

Training My New Family

I went to the door and sat down to begin testing the man and the woman to see how quickly they could learn. I guess they didn't see me so I let out a soft howl and stared at them. What results! Immediately, she came to the door and opened it for me to go out.

I went straight to the woods to dig a hole and go to the 'potty', as they had called it. When I was ready to come in, I scratched on the glass doors and the man came to let me in. Boy they were fast learners.

I might be able to train them faster than I had expected, I thought. Locating the smell of the cat food, I figured I would impress the man once more. I sat in front of the door to a closet. He opened the door to get the food. Once more he was delighted with how smart I was. It was simply a matter of following your nose. No big deal, but I let him think it was.

He opened a can of food, while she was getting me some milk. He put the food in the usual spot on the deck. That just wouldn't do! So I smelled the food, turned my nose up, and went back into the kitchen. I sat down next to the living room and thought *this* spot would do nicely for eating. After all it may be raining some day and I'm not a cat to get wet in order to eat.

After a short wait, I scratched on the floor. The woman told the man she thought I wanted the food inside. He mumbled, then went and got the food. He placed it on the floor where I was sitting and where she had placed the milk.

Since I needed to know where everything was in my new home, I went to explore the downstairs. When my curiosity was satisfied I jumped up on the bed and, putting my head on a pillow, I fell asleep.

The sound of the man laughing woke me up. I heard him tell his wife that Smokie had adopted a bed for himself. She said I looked adorable with my head on the pillow.

When I awoke, I had the urge to be sure that there was still a place to hide and to sleep in the barn, just in case I decided to go there for a nap. When I climbed the hill by the side of the road, I found everything still the same in the barn.

Past the barn was a dirt covered lot. I walked on toward the other end of the open lot and climbed over a pile of railroad ties to look for mice. I didn't find any mice, but I did see a big wiggly bug. I went into a stalking position and after giving a few wiggles myself, I jumped on this creature like a wild tiger. It sure didn't smell very good and it was rather hard—just not the kind of bug a Manx cat would eat. I found myself next to the woods at the end of the lot, and decided to investigate. When I came to the edge of a road, I noticed the cabin where I had found the cat that looked like me. I started towards it, but I was scared by the noise of a car. I sprang into the air and, turning while still in midair, I landed in the underbrush by the side of the road. The car slowed down and stopped just past me. The door opened and a man got out. He walked slowly in my direction. Just as I was about to dart away, I heard the man call my name, "Smokie, come here boy." Yes, I saw it was the man at my new home, so I walked over to him. "Are you lost?" he asked. "Daddy will take you home." This was the second time he had said Daddy. Well, if that's what he wants to be called, I'll call him *Daddy*. He swooped me up and, opening the car door, put me on the front seat beside him. It seemed safe enough inside the car.

Daddy's voice was caring and soothing as he told me it was okay. Looking out the window, I could see that the road led past the open lot, the entrance to the dirt road, past the barn on the left, and down the hill. Seeing all of this, I now knew where I was and how I got there. The car turned into the driveway of the brown house, and I was back *home*.

Daddy opened the door and let me jump out all by myself. I was glad to see that he knew I didn't have to be carried. I followed him to the front door and went with him inside. I went straight to the kitchen. Sure enough there was food and water on the floor, just for me.

After that I knew that if I needed help, my Daddy would come to my rescue, although I was still not quite sure whether his appearance was a coincidence or not. I had had enough roaming for one day, so I went downstairs, jumped on the sofa and, putting my head on the edge of a pillow, went to sleep.

I must have been more tired than I thought. When I awoke it was getting light outside. The door to the workshop was slightly ajar. Pushing it open gave me access to the covered hole or, as Daddy called it, a port-o-door. I was now able to go outside all by myself.

I went up to the front of the house, where a squirrel was coming down the big oak tree. Instantly, I went into a stalking mode. The squirrel paused near the bottom of the tree and looked in my direction. He must have seen me, because he began a loud chattering, looked squarely at me, and waved his tail tauntingly. He appeared to be daring me to try to catch him. He leaped to the ground, ran a few feet, and turned to look at me. He chattered a challenge again. As I started to slink forward, he moved a few more feet. It seemed as though he knew how far away he had to stay in order to be able to outrun me. "Well, I'll show him," I said out loud. My strong hind legs let me leap a good distance before I started chasing him. This large leap let me cover more distance than he had figured. He ran so fast it seemed like he was able to fly. As I reached for that waving tail, he leaped about four feet up the tulip poplar in front of the house. I lunged up the tree and was only able to swat at the very end of his tail. Without a breath he was halfway up the tree and out of reach. i think my leap had really surprised him. Little did I know how long he would enjoy this game of catch me if you can. Every time I appeared in the front yard he would tease me, running between trees just slow enough to get me to chase him.

Being winded myself, I started down toward the fountain. It was lighter now and I was beginning to get hungry. Out of nowhere, a big red dog came running across the front yard. Before I could reach the steps to the deck he had gotten just in back of me and was barking loudly. I had to take the offense once more. If I didn't, he would surely be able to grab me on my back or neck. I turned and growled as loudly and fiercely as I could. He stopped dead in his tracks and almost fell down in an attempt to back up. For what seemed like an eternity, I would growl and he would lunge back and forth barking and growling all the while. We had made enough noise that I thought that Daddy would hear and come to help.

Sure enough, the door to the house opened and Daddy ran out. When he saw the big, red dog, he got between us and began chasing the dog out of our yard. Having come out in a hurry, Daddy had left the door open just enough for me to squeeze through. I hid under the couch where I could settle down and catch my breath. I hadn't seen this dog before and figured that he must come out early in the morning. So, I thought that I better not go out in the front yard at that time again.

When my Daddy came in, he looked under the couch and quietly told me over and over that it was okay for me to come out. When I came out, he picked me up and said, "Mommy and Daddy will always take care of you." Well, I guess I was to call the woman *Mommy.* That was fine with me. I calmly jumped up on the sofa and fell asleep.

By afternoon, I was awake and my thoughts returned to the squirrel. Maybe, just maybe, I could climb that oak tree and surprise the squirrel. I went to the porch door and looked at Mommy. She opened the door and watched me go to the front yard right by the oak tree. Leaping up a short way, I dug the claws of all four of my paws into the bark. Pushing with my hind legs and digging my front claws in a little higher, it was not a problem to climb the tree. In order for this to work, I had to spread my front paws out around the tree as far as I could reach. Up, up, up I went until I could sit on the large branch that spread out to the house. Pausing on the branch, I regained my confidence and strength. Renewing my upward climb, I was soon three more sets of branches higher. Satisfied that I could climb the oak tree, I figured that I might as well back down. Uh oh. This tree was too large for me to get my legs far enough around to be able to back down. So I froze on the limb and tried to call for help by thinking real hard. I figured I might be able to send a message to Daddy. Within a short time, I could hear my name being called. My Daddy saw me looking kind of forlorn, and went around back to get a tall ladder. He climbed up to the first branch and called, "come on to Daddy Smokie." But, there was nothing for me to stand on if I went toward him. Did he want me to jump down? It was too far! With fear taking over, I climbed up to a higher branch. I didn't know why he seemed frustrated.

He climbed as high as he could on the ladder and then stretched up to grab me. When Daddy pulled me down and over to him, I dug my claws into his coat to hold on like I had held on to the tree. He began slowly down the ladder. I felt he had a tight grip on me, so I eased my hold on him. Before long we were safe on the ground. He carried me back into the house, where he and Mommy got me settled down so I could eat my dinner.

Some time later, when Mommy and Daddy were getting ready for bed, I figured their bed should be my bed also. So I sprang from the floor onto the bed and laid down right between them. They seemed surprised but happy to have my company.

There must be a special way to sleep in this kind of bed. So, I looked at Daddy and, seeing he was on his back, I rolled over on *my* back and went to sleep. When he turned on his side, I turned on *my* side and my right paw fell over his neck. I felt very safe and very comfortable and, as my head leaned against his head, I fell asleep. I realized that we hadn't been this close since that first night on the floor. It became a habit for me to copy sleeping in the same positions as my Daddy. As a matter of fact, Mommy took many pictures of these various positions throughout our years together. The one on my back they called my "otter" position.

Yes, I bonded even more closely with my Daddy. It wasn't very long before we could sense where each of us was and, as I settled into my new home, they were becoming much better at knowing what I wanted. I realized that, on some days, my Daddy would leave in the morning and return that afternoon just before dinner. He would be home all day on what they called weekends and during special holidays. I didn't understand about the meaning of holidays, but I'm glad they had them. On those days I could be with my Daddy all day. During the days, when he was away, I would feel a little lonely. At those times, I would remember my mother and sister. I began thinking that another cat would be a lot of company for me when Mommy and Daddy were busy or gone somewhere.

As fate would have it, one morning I went out to explore the path through the woods. I heard something moving very softly. Was it a dog? I didn't think so. It was moving far too daintily. I crouched behind some undergrowth and waited. Coming into view was a pretty little girl cat. She had a beautiful black coat and yellow-green eyes. She saw me and paused. Remembering how the pretty white cat in the house on the hill had lunged at me, I was cautious, since there wasn't a door between us. We both moved slowly toward each other. As cats do, we smelled each other. In this way we could recognize each other's scent later. When she rubbed against me, I realized I had found a friend. We kissed each other's nose, and I told her about the house and family I had found at the other end of the path. She couldn't believe there was always food handy. She told me she hadn't eaten for awhile and that she had been chased away by people and dogs at other houses. So I told her to follow me to my home for a meal. As we neared the house, I realized I hadn't thought about whether Mommy or Daddy would accept her. Well, I'll just put on my confident attitude and march right inside

At the door of the living room, I told her that when the door opened, we would both run straight ahead to the food. Luckily, Mommy was nearby and saw me at the door. As she opened it, we both ran by quickly to the kitchen. "Oh my! What is this?" Mommy asked. When she saw how hungry the little girl was, Mommy left her alone to eat. To let Mommy know that I was happy with my new friend, I rubbed against the little girl and she rubbed against me.

There wasn't any canned food out, so I walked over to the pantry door. I was able to get Mommy's attention by staring at the door. She understood and got out some Sheba cat food. The plate was hardly on the floor, when the little girl began gobbling it down, completely devouring all of it. At that point Mommy said, "Well I guess you have a girlfriend. We'll see what to do about her when Daddy gets home."

Her tummy full the little girl let me know that she wanted to take a nap. She cautiously followed me downstairs. Since this was all new to her, I showed her the downstairs and then went to a bed in the bedroom. When I hopped up on the bed, she followed me. After kneading and smelling the bedspread, she snuggled against a blanket and, using it as a pillow, she fell asleep. Not being as tired as the little girl, I peered out of the window. There didn't seem to be anything of much interest outside. I figured I had better stay here, because she might wake up and be frightened in a new place. I moved over to the fluffy blanket and began kneading it as I moved around in a circle to get in just the right position. I laid down on the blanket with my head beside her. With a new friend I fell asleep within a short time.

When Daddy arrived home, the door opening upstairs scared the little girl so that for a moment she didn't know where she was. I assured her it was okay and I reminded her that I had been able to get her food, a nice place to sleep, and had taken care of her very well so far. So, she settled down and slowly followed me upstairs. She cringed on the steps when she saw Daddy.

I went back and kissed her. Rubbing against her side reassured her and let Daddy see that she was my friend. Mommy explained what had happened as she put down another plate of food.

"Shall we keep Smokie's new friend?", Daddy asked. After a discussion, they decided to let her stay. I ran over to her, but she wasn't quite sure what this meant. "If we are going to keep her what shall we call her?" Daddy asked.

"*Sheba*," Mommy said. "Yes, she looks just like the picture on the package of Sheba cat food." I tried to explain the new name to my friend. She agreed that if it meant a home, safety, food, and me for a friend, she would answer to the name of Sheba. The training of my new family was at an all time high with the acceptance of Sheba.

At that time I began to really enjoy my life and family. I started having fun showing Sheba the barn and the house on the hill where the woman with the broom lived. After I showed her the road to the lot across from the small house on the hill, I let her see the way down the big hill to our home. Then I showed her the woods next to the house and all around the yard. Sheba quickly learned how to use the port-o-doors to get into the workshop or on the porch. She felt safe at her new home!

Chapter 6

Adventures at My New home

I had gotten into a routine of going to the front window to watch for Daddy.

I seemed to sense the time he'd come home. When he arrived, I would go to the door and greet my Daddy with a big mroow. If I was outside, I went to the front of the house to greet him near the driveway. This gave me a great deal of pleasure, as it did him. Sheba thought this was tiresome and silly. Besides, Daddy was *my* friend, while she was closer to Mommy.

I didn't mind if she got attention from Daddy as long as she didn't overdo it. If she did I, as the dominant male, would stare her down, swat her gently, or in some way get her to be submissive to me. I got a lot of pleasure from chasing her around the house. However, sometimes she got tired of my bossiness and didn't like my bullying. That's when she would stop, glare at me, or swat me back. Her bright, yellow-green eyes behind that dark, black fur coat would scare anyone. That's how I learned to speak Russian, giving out with a whiny, high pitched nyet, nyet. (It sounded more like a no, no, please, in a begging manner). Quite often that would make her feel sorry for me or she thought I was being submissive, so she would turn around and walk off. That's when I would jump on her and knock her down. Sometimes this restored my authority. But, if she wasn't in the best of moods, she would swat me and give me a glare, nasty enough to scare me into leaving her alone.

One day we were both on the porch, when she started to playfully chase me. As I ran to get away, I instinctively jumped onto the post of the porch and climbed up to the open rafters. I found that I could balance myself on them and step from one rafter to the next one easily. There was a dark opening at the end of the rafters over the screen door, which just had to be investigated! Peeking in I could see inside the overhang from the roof. I went in slowly, to be sure it would hold me. It did, so I moved farther in. There was a light to my left coming through an opening. Peeking through the opening I saw a room that I hadn't seen before. Since this was my home, I needed to know about this room, so I slipped through the opening and went in. One window allowed more than enough light for me to see clearly.

It was awfully quiet. Then I heard a clawing noise. A dark animal was coming out of the opening. To my surprise, I saw that it was Sheba. Whew! Was I relieved. Boy, with her sharp claws she had been able to climb the post to the overhang just like me. I guess I had underestimated her abilities. I was glad, because now I had a friend to help me explore. Together we discovered some screens, lots of boxes, a few rugs, and all sorts of things we could use for hiding. On the other side of the room was another overhang. We both went down into it and moved toward the light. At the end of the overhang, I could see outside. In front of me was the branch that went back to the oak tree in front of the house. The part of the branch near the house was too small to hold my weight and there wasn't room to get a running start for a leap to the larger part of the branch. Besides, I had gotten stuck up that tree before. I thought I had better leave well enough alone. I explained this to Sheba so she wouldn't try to jump. We had to climb higher than we did from the other overhang, in order to get back into the room.

Looking across from the window, we saw a hallway leading to an open door. Inside was a big room with windows at each end. There were lots of things to see in there and plenty of room to move around. I jumped on a chest under a window and landed on a soft rug. I could see a tulip poplar and several other trees from up there. I could also see a fenced in garden on part of the wooded lot next to the road. I could see a big house across the street and a smaller house almost hidden by trees. Sheba jumped up on the chest with me, and she let me know that there was a blue colored cat staying at the house hidden in the trees. She told me that he had a terrible temper. Well, he was outside and not a threat to us inside. The rug on the chest was comfortable, so we decided it was a good time to take a nap. The windows allowed just enough sun through the leaves of the tree for it to be comfortably warm.

The sun going down made the room cooler, reminding us it was time for dinner. We jumped down and, seeing a set of steps, decided they would be easier to use rather than climbing back down to the porch. However, at the bottom of the stairs the door was closed. We could see light under the door and we could hear Mommy and Daddy. Since Sheba could meow very loudly, I let her call. It wasn't long before a surprised Mommy and Daddy opened the door to the attic. It was quite awhile before Mommy or Daddy could figure out how we had gotten up there with the door closed. It wasn't until later, when Daddy saw me climb the porch post, that he knew how we were able to get into the attic.

After dinner, we went downstairs and noticed the workshop door open. We went out the port-o-door and up to the front yard. All of a sudden, we saw another cat coming up the slope from the road. Sheba recognized it as the bluish cat with the bad temper. He was a Russian Blue cat we heard Daddy say later. This was our yard, and I decided that he should be made aware of that fact and should be chased out of our yard. I was sure that once he got a close look at me he would leave. As I approached boldly, he took a stance and let out a nasty cat warning. When I kept going toward him, I forgot all about my short front legs, which was a bad mistake. His paws reached my face with a big slap. When I didn't get scratched, I figured that this cat didn't have any claws. Again, I was sure I could chase him away because he couldn't scratch me.

He ran to the bushes beside the porch. I chased him and dove into the bushes so I could jump on him and use the claws on my hind feet to teach him a lesson. To my surprise and dismay, I felt a sharp pain on my head. He jumped back as I howled in pain. He had *bitten* my head and it was bleeding. As he moved away I flew to the port-o-door into the workshop.

Right then I needed help from Daddy. He and Mommy saw my head wound when I got upstairs. They wrapped me in a towel, put me in the car, and took me to the doctor. It must have been a bad cut, because the doctor stuck something in it to stop the pain and then sewed it up. I heard him tell Mommy and Daddy that he had given me five stitches. I had to take some pills every day and stay quiet for a week. The bite healed, and I had learned a valuable lesson. I shouldn't be too quick to act before I know all of the facts. It was even more humiliating when Sheba said she had given him her really nasty look, and had chased him out of the yard while I was getting better. I told you she could look really mean. I guess I was lucky she was my friend.

Sheba and I had fun playing hide and seek a game we continued to play for most of our lives. I also discovered that it was fun to climb the wide posts that held the deck up. From there I could walk on the beams that also helped support the deck. That was something Sheba couldn't do, even with her sharp claws. This gave me a place to escape or go to, when I just wanted to be left alone.

Now, I had always stayed out of the neighbor cat's yard, as a sort of cat courtesy, you know. However, one day on my way to explore the driveway across the road, I upset him. I didn't know why, because it wasn't his territory, but then, it wasn't my territory either. Actually, it was probably the territory of the little dog that lived in the house at the end of that driveway. As a matter of fact, the little dog and I had learned to tolerate each other, because his Daddy would come over to talk to my Daddy. Anyway, it seemed like it would be all right for me to go over to his driveway.

I had just gotten into the driveway, when I heard the neighbor's cat send a warning call behind me. Remembering my experience with the blue cat, I decided to use the ploy that always worked with Sheba. I crouched down and howled my now famous, nyet......nyet...nyet, in a pleading manner. It worked. He strolled by me into the driveway. Then I jumped up, leaped on his back and scratched him with my strong hind legs. Then I returned to my own yard. From that point on the neighbor's cat and I maintained a mutual respect, which we agreed to silently. This respect worked out well, as we never did challenge each other again. Thus, our first upset ended in a pleasant compromise that made life happier.

Sheba was spending more and more time inside, instead of exploring with me. She had eaten her way into becoming a fat cat, instead of the little girl I had brought home. We were still just as close, but it was becoming harder for her to keep up with me.

When my Daddy was home I enjoyed playing hide and seek with him. I would crouch behind a bush and jump out to surprise him when he was looking for me. If he was weeding, I would dig beside him and bite weeds to pull them up for him. Sometimes, he would rake leaves into a big pile, and I would jump in the middle of them, grabbing at them over and over. I would keep this up until he had gotten them all in a bag or raked over to a mulch pile by the woods. It was on an occasion like this, that I would move next to his leg and give him a little love bump with my high, rounded rump. Knowing why I did this, sometimes Daddy would call me his *little love bump*. Whenever he would sing, "Oh, a little love bump, that's what he is, bump, bump," I would give him a big bump with my rump.

One day, I was studying the hummingbirds at the feeders hanging from the deck in the back. Sheba and Mommy were watching me through the glass doors in the living room. After watching the hummingbirds I noticed that, when they weren't chasing each other, they made regular swoops down over the stair landing and back up to the feeders. So, as one hummingbird left the feeder, I leaped to the spot where he would be when he swooped down. Sure enough, he was there at the same time I was. I was able to grab him in mid-air. I held him gently in my mouth and was going to give him to Mommy as a gift, when she opened the door and scolded, "Let him go." As he flew away, she thanked me, but told me, "No, No, No." I got the message—she didn't want me to bother the hummingbirds. Being a quick learner, and wanting to always please Mommy, I didn't bother them again. I think this surprised her.

I knew that I wasn't supposed to bother the hummingbirds, but no one had mentioned the little, yellow bees that also ate the sugar water. They were even more of a challenge. I waited a few days, studying the flying patterns of the bees. During this time, Daddy had taken off the screen door into the porch and had replaced it with a new one. He had laid the old one against the back of the house on the deck.

I noticed that the bees only flew to the feeder, drank, and flew away without a swooping pattern like the hummingbirds. I knew that if I wanted to catch one of the bees, I would have to climb close enough to swat one while he was on the feeder. I jumped up on the railing beside the feeder near the steps. I also knew I'd have to be sure, to knock it out or it would fly after me and sting me. I had seen bees do this to people at the cabin, where I was born.

As I sat motionless, a bee flew down to the feeder. Waiting until he was busy drinking, I gave him a swat with my paw. He went down but not out. I figured I had better run in the port-o-door to the safety of the porch. But, as I reached the port-o-door, I heard a couple of bees flying toward me. I knew that I could be stung on the rump if I started through the port-o-door. Where would I be safe? Moving as quickly as I was thinking, I ran behind the screen door that was leaning against the house. It worked—the bees landed on the screen and didn't have sense enough to go around to the end. After awhile the bees gave up and left. Then I dashed for the porch and went in. Safe again, after another exciting adventure.

Once, when the cat next door told me that there was a strange cat coming through the woods by his yard, we decided to work together and let this stranger know he was in our territory and that he was not welcome. Going to the edge of the woods, we gave our warnings. He howled loudly and I gave my hearty Manx growl. The stranger howled back. We continued to get louder and louder. It was loud enough to bring my Daddy and his neighbor friend out to see what was going on. After listening to our total howling, the neighbor called his cat and picked him up. Seeing my Daddy gave me a renewed courage. I started toward the strange cat, but Daddy grabbed me, and turned toward our house. I was so stirred up that I gave a half growl, half howl so loud it could be heard all through the woods. It scared the strange cat so badly, he took off like a shot. I'll bet he's still running. To keep me from jumping down and chasing the strange cat, my Daddy had to hold me tightly as he carried me home. All the way home he told me he loved me. Slowly I settled down, and realized he was concerned for my safety. What a wonderful Daddy.

I must have been dirty and sweaty, because when I got in the house Mommy said that I needed a bath. While I always felt better afterward, a bath wasn't in my realm of enjoyment. I would sit quietly in the tub full of water until I was washed and rinsed. When I was wrapped in towels, I let out a garbling noise, to let Mommy know that I didn't appreciate a forced bath. Right after a bath, I always got a treat. That was Mommy's way of thanking me for sitting in the laundry tub like a gentleman. Sometimes, she would get a paper bag or a box out to play with me and Sheba.

I remember the night some white flakes began coming down from the sky. Daddy said it was snow. The next morning the ground was covered with it. Daddy put on his coat and gloves and we went out the front door. My thick, double coat kept me dry and warm. As I stepped into the snow I sank a little, then stopped. It was soft and fluffy. I had such fun tossing the snow into the air. I would grab it in both paws, bite at it or toss it up. From then on, I looked forward to seeing it snow.

Chapter 7

A Move to the Shore

I began noticing that Daddy was bringing home lots of boxes. There were too many for him to have gotten them for Sheba and me to play in. Mommy and Daddy would pack them full of things and stack them in the hall. He would take them with him when he left on Monday mornings, but he didn't come back until Friday afternoons. This really messed up my schedule of greeting him each afternoon. I would go to the door, then to the window sill and watch for him. What was going on? More and more things went out but they never came back with Daddy.

Then one weekend Daddy brought a big truck home and the neighbors and members of our family helped load furniture into the truck. At one point I remember seeing a chair on the front stoop and climbed in it. Maybe they would see that I didn't want everything moved out. I don't care for too much change at one time. The chair was loaded with me in it. I jumped down and ran back to the door of my home.

When the truck was full, we went back in and ate some lunch. Daddy left in the truck and Mommy loaded some food and clothes in the car. Then she put Sheba and me in a carrier and placed us on the back seat of the car. When we were on our way, she opened the doors on both of our carriers, so we could move freely inside the car.

After riding for a long while, I heard the noisy sounds of many cars and trucks. I hid my head in my blanket until it felt like the car was going uphill. Well now I had to see what was happening, so I left my carrier, and looked out the window. Everything seemed to be moving so fast that it made me feel dizzy. Looking out of the back window, everything slowed down and I could see a line of cars behind us on a bridge over lots of water. On the other side of the water, the land was flat. Where were the hills I had been used to seeing? After a few hours, we pulled into a parking lot surrounded by tall buildings that all looked alike. I went back into my carrier to wait until I was back home. Sheba hadn't even come out of her's. Mommy closed our doors, and Daddy came over to help her carry us into one of the buildings next to a small bridge over a narrow stream.

We were carried up a set of stairs, and there our carriers were opened so Sheba and I could investigate the new place. Behind the carriers was a spiral staircase that went up to an opening. Curiosity sent me up the stairs to a loft, where I could see down into a living room. The carriers were right below me and I could see Sheba cautiously coming out of her's. She wasn't as brave as me, so I went back downstairs to help her relax. I told her that it would be a good idea for us to do some more exploring together. Going around a counter we saw a large set of glass doors that opened onto a deck. There was a table with a glass top and four chairs. As I jumped into a chair beside the table, I could see out the window. Below was a small stream, grass, trees, and more buildings.

Hurrying around the counter, we saw the steps we had come up and straight ahead of us was a hallway. Since we knew where the steps led, we went down the hallway. In front of us was a large bedroom with a bathroom on the right. Just inside the bedroom door was a big closet. Looking in I could smell clothes like Mommy's and Daddy's. I wondered why their clothes would be here? Were we staying? Sheba and I didn't think so, since there were still clothes and furniture back home.

In the bedroom was a bed larger than we had seen before. Sheba and I sprang up on the bed and found that it was very comfortable. From there I could see the stream below that I had also seen from the dining room window. Sheba had climbed off the bed, so I joined her to continue exploring. At the end of the hallway were two doors that opened into two more bedrooms. On the far side of these bedrooms were sliding glass doors. Daddy came in behind us and opened the door. There was a small balcony outside with a wall and railing. From there we could see the parking lot, our car, and steps leading up to several other buildings that looked just like the one we were in. There were shrubs below us, but they seemed a little too far down for us to jump, so we went back inside. Mommy had put some food down for us at the end of the kitchen counter. After eating, Daddy showed us that he had opened the doors to the deck. Sheba and I cautiously stepped out. The railing around the deck was wide enough for a nice view of the whole place.

The parking lot was on the other side of the stream. How could I get across? Then I remembered the bridge I had seen on the way in. A tree hung over close to the railing on the deck, but the tiny branches were too small to hold me. Thank goodness, I thought, when I saw the litter box in the corner of the deck. I hadn't any idea where there was dirt for me to dig a hole for a potty. Around home I knew plenty of places in the woods, but for now a litter box would do. It had been a long tiring day. I fell asleep on the couch and Sheba slept on a cushion Mommy had put on the floor.

When I awoke, I saw the door to a cabinet under the kitchen counter was ajar so I pushed it open and went in. Inside I could see light around another door on the other side. Climbing over a few pots, I found the other door was closed. Suddenly, I heard Daddy close the door I had come in. Oh well, I figured he would open it and let me out in a little while, so I laid down to wait and I fell asleep.

I awoke hearing Daddy and Mommy calling my name over and over. I said to myself, "shucks all they had to do was open the cabinet door and I would be glad to come out." I heard her asking Daddy if I could have climbed down the tree. He ran down the steps and I could hear him calling me. Didn't he remember closing the door? He came back in and told Mommy that he didn't see me anywhere.

Enough is enough! I guess I needed to use my bonding senses to send Daddy a message. That was harder than I thought, because he was so upset over me being lost in these new surroundings he couldn't hear my silent call.

They looked for me in all the closets, under beds, under furniture, and up in the loft. When they sat down to think, I sent another mental message to them. Sure enough, Daddy opened the door and there I sat. Mommy and Daddy were overjoyed to find me. I guess that was my first adventure on the Shore. I didn't know then that I was going to have to learn about more homes than I wanted to.

Just as Sheba and I were getting familiar with the place, we were packed up and put in the car to travel once more. The doors to our carriers were opened so we could look out of the car windows. I couldn't remember for sure, but it seemed like we were going back the same way we came. After about an hour on the road we stopped. I saw a vegetable stand and some long buildings so, when the door opened, I jumped over the seat and out the door. After a few feet, I realized nothing looked familiar. As I started to run, Daddy grabbed me and put me back in the car. He told Mommy I needed to be put in the carrier before opening the door next time. It was scary jumping out in a place I didn't know—another adventure on the Shore. After putting some vegetables in the trunk, we were on our way again. Lying in the back window, I could see some familiar places we had passed on the way to the Shore, but there was nothing comforting to see. Exhausted, I fell asleep on the floor of the back seat.

All of a sudden I was awakened by some familiar smells. From the window, I saw familiar pine trees near home, so I let out a loud mroow. Mommy and Daddy thought I was very smart to recognize where we were. I got so much praise that I decided to howl every time we got near home. Whenever I went to the cat doctor or any-where, I gave a howl as we reached a familiar scent, sight, or sound that meant we were near home, and I always got lots of praise for this accomplishment. Back home at last.

However, too soon, it was back to the Shore again. It was during that visit to the Shore, I surprised Daddy one evening as he was eating dinner. I was in the chair next to him, when he took a drink of milk from his glass. Boy did it look good. Since I'm part of the family and so close to him, I didn't think it was wrong to hop onto the table and take a drink from his glass. While I wasn't scolded, it was made clear that was not an acceptable behavior. In order to maintain my independence and expand the training of Mommy and Daddy, I laid on the table as they ate.

I pushed this control a little bit further, by sitting in the chair next to Daddy across the table from Mommy. I stared at them until they realized that I wanted to eat with my family.

Sure enough, they put part of a can of my food on a plate on the table in front of me. I really enjoyed eating at the table with them.

By now I had been allowed to go outside with Daddy or Mommy. When I went out of sight behind the bushes or on the side of the condo, they would whistle the same little whistle that they used to get each other's attention. This was sort of a family whistle. Hearing it, I would return to them. They thought this was great and I received praise for accepting another family tradition. From the very first time, I learned to respond to this whistle as well as to my name.

One day, on our return to the Shore we took the last of the clothing and furniture. I guess the *condo*, as they called it, was to become our new home. After many walks with Daddy around the condo's parking lot and beside the stream to the back of the condo, I felt secure. It was then that I was allowed out alone or with Sheba. She never went very far, but we both enjoyed lying under the front shrubs. There was a clear spot under them where we were hidden from sight. It was shaded and always cool and comfy. On the side were shrubs and trees we could climb or hide behind. We felt like we were beginning to get more settled in our new place on the Shore.

At our old home, we had a much bigger yard in which to explore. So I felt it was time to roam a little farther from the condo. This made sense to me. Besides, I was curious to know what was beyond the fence. Was there a barn somewhere down the road? I wondered if there were places to visit like we had at our old home.

When we went to our new cat doctors, we found them very nice, because while we usually saw one particular doctor, there were others who helped take care of us. They even called our home to ask how we were doing. I had developed a cough, so Mommy took me to the doctor's again. The doctor placed me in front of a machine and took a picture. After several tests, it was discovered that I had asthma. The doctor was also concerned about a dark shadow which showed up in the picture of my lungs. As a result, I was taken to a *special* doctor and spent a few days in the hospital. The tests showed that I had a kidney behind my lungs, but that the kidney was working fine.

When I got back home, I had forgotten all about exploring a bigger territory. Sheba surprised me and Mommy and Daddy one day, when we were outside. A big dog from across the parking lot came out and ran toward us. Sheba was so scared that she leaped on top of the railing beneath the small balcony. Then she did what seemed impossible. She climbed straight up the wood siding to our balcony. Even with my strong hind legs, I couldn't do that. Mommy ran upstairs to let her inside. I had jumped up on the railing and was growling fiercely at the dog. As Daddy talked to him he starting wagging his tail. His owners came and put him on a leash and told Daddy they hadn't seen Sheba and me. I knew that Daddy and I, working together, had stopped the dog!

Poor Sheba was still upset when I went inside. I was hungry and my getting her to eat with me took her mind off the dog. After all that excitement we needed to take a relaxing nap. But, this time we both wanted to get as far away from the outside as possible, so we went up to the loft where we were up high and out of sight. Besides, two cushions had been put in the loft, just for us to sleep on.

We must have really been more exhausted than we realized, because it was morning before Sheba and I woke up. Yesterday was past; it was time for me to get back to exploring a larger territory to claim as mine. After eating a small breakfast, I went to the downstairs door to go out. Sheba didn't want to go out so I headed for the bridge, crossed over, went through the parking lot, squeezed under the fence, and went quickly down the sidewalk. I thought if I didn't hurry, Daddy might try to stop me from going.

As I passed the end of the fence I could see a row of small houses in the middle of some trees. I didn't see anyone watching me as I dashed to the first house. There were lots of little places to sneak around and under. It was so exciting, I didn't realize I was moving farther away from home.

On the other side of these houses was an open yard that went all the way around a building. Running to the side of the building, I paused to look, listen and smell. Moving around front, I could see a larger house with a porch. I scooted over to the porch and went under. It smelled like there were people inside but I didn't hear anyone. Beyond the house was an empty lot overgrown with trees and bushes. It was a good place to hide, because it was similar to where I used to hide at my old *home.*

After a short rest, I discovered a small dirt drive with a lot of different sized trailer homes. This probably could become part of my territory also. Moving under and between the trailers, I suddenly realized I was not near anything that I recognized in order to get back home. I was lost! At first I was too scared to think clearly. That's it....think. It had worked before, so I concentrated on Daddy as hard as I could.

It seemed like hours before I heard that familiar whistle of Daddy's. I ran out and greeted him with a big mrooow. He scooped me up, hugged me, and carried me home. It had worked again! Boy was I lucky to have bonded with a Daddy that could sense my thoughts, and that I had learned to recognize the family whistle.

At first I wanted to get down; after all, I could walk by myself. Then I heard some dogs barking behind us, but with Daddy holding me I felt very brave. So I growled at the dogs but, luckily, they were too far back to hear. I guess it was a good thing Daddy was holding me because there were three of them running back and forth across the street like hunting dogs searching a field. They were moving too fast for me to have been able to outrun all three.

Whew! We were home at last. When we went inside, Sheba was there for me to tell her all about my adventure. I told Sheba I had decided the territory close to the condo was enough for me. I never wanted to go that far again without some woods to hide in or some trees to climb.

Everything went along fine for some time, but I really missed having a home with a port-o-door and a yard. Then one day, some strange people came in and walked all over the condo. Sheba and I hid in the loft while they talked with Mommy and Daddy. After they left, the boxes began coming in and packing began again. As the boxes were filled they were taken out a few at a time. No furniture was moved this time, however. Then I remembered that the furniture was already in the condo when we moved in. What was going on? We soon found out we were moving again, but not back to our old *home* though.

Instead, we moved into a townhouse on a lake that had two floors with a front and back door. There was a screened porch, where Sheba and I could look at the lake. It was getting late, so we ate dinner and went back out on the porch to sleep for the first night. It was too late to start getting to know our surroundings.

The next morning I figured I had better get to know the place pretty quickly. Daddy let me out the front door, following close behind. On the left was a closed in shower. Going under the short door I found a bench, where I could hide easily and quickly. Coming back out I smelled the flowers and shrubs next to a walk. Another place I could hide if I stayed low to the ground. Ahead of me, was a parking lot and Daddy's car. This place didn't seem like it would be too hard for me to learn my way around. I ran to the right, where there were more entrances to townhouses. Running back, I went to the door where Daddy was still standing. Knowing that he was still there made me feel safer. With my confidence renewed, I smelled all of the scents in order to be able to recognize our front door, since they all looked alike.

At the end of the row of townhouses there was a wide clear area with a path leading into the woods. Naturally, off I went down the path, climbing on fallen trees high enough for me to be safe and yet see in every direction. I jumped down just as Daddy entered the path. He was calling me, but I thought he was playing hide and seek, so I stayed low, ready to spring out and scare him. As I listened carefully for his footsteps, it suddenly became quiet.

Instead of coming toward me, he had gone back out of the path and disappeared. I walked towards the back of several town-houses. The smells became familiar so I knew I was getting near the porch on our new home. The screened door was ajar and inside I could hear Daddy telling Mommy that I had disappeared into the woods. They were both getting ready to go out the front door when Sheba ran over to me meowing loudly. They saw her and me at the same time. Picking me up, they hugged me to show how glad they were that I was safe. Quite a few months went by with Sheba and I exploring the woods, the edge of the lake, and playing hide and seek.

One day I was out front with Daddy when the people next door came out with a medium-sized, brown dog. I hid under Daddy's car, just in case. Looking from behind one of the tires, I saw the dog going toward my Daddy. Being jealous, I leaped on the dog's back, scratching him with the claws on my strong hind legs. When I heard him howl in pain, I jumped off and scooted up the tree that was in front of our townhouse. The man took his dog back into the house and Daddy came over to the tree to coax me down, but it was a tall tree with no branches near the ground. I thought that Daddy would surely get his ladder and get me down just like he did when I was stuck up the oak tree at our old home. Instead, I heard him tell Mommy he didn't have a ladder. He talked and talked to me. But I was so worried, I couldn't understand what he was trying to get me to do. Then he sat down and began to think and think until I was able to read his mind, and I climbed down backwards like a pole climber. Being able to share our thoughts had helped us again.

Chapter 8

My Final Move—A Real Home Again

Well, it seemed as though we were just getting adjusted to the townhouse, when the boxes started coming in again. It didn't seem like there was very much for Mommy and Daddy to move anymore. I never did see that big truck again that took all the furniture away from the old home. After the phone rang one day, while Mommy was out, Daddy put me in the car to go for a ride with him. We didn't go very far before we turned onto a new road, where *nothing* was familiar. As we went farther down this new road, we pulled up in front of a house.

It was then that I saw the same truck that had taken our furniture away a long time ago. It backed into the driveway of this strange house. I could see lots of trees, next to the house. Then Mommy pulled up in front of us with Sheba. Daddy took me up to Mommy's car and put me inside with Sheba. When I asked Sheba what she knew, she told me that she didn't know what was happening any more than I did.

After the men in the truck had taken all of the furniture into the house, the long truck left. Daddy came and got me; Mommy got Sheba; and they carried us inside the house. Sheba and I were allowed to get down and explore the new smelling house. In the living room, we found the same sofa and chairs that had been in the old home. If we were going to stay in this house, it would be easy for

us to adjust, since all of our furniture was there. Except for the new-
ness, it seemed more like home. At the back of the den upstairs was
a glass sliding door that Daddy opened for Sheba and me. Sheba
wasn't nearly as afraid, now that we had our original furniture back.
We went out on a small deck, from where we could see some water
and a lot with trees next door.

We looked as far as we could see and took in all of the new
smells. There were a few ducks just like the ones we had seen at the
condo. The lot with trees looked interesting, but there wasn't any
way to climb down from the deck so we went back inside and
downstairs. We went through the kitchen to a screened porch.
Mommy called us out there to see that she had put our food on the
porch. We ate and then Mommy showed us a port-o-door from the
porch to an outside deck. We both remembered how to use a port-
o-door, so we went out to look around. Sheba was now beside me
walking toward the lot, and Mommy and Daddy were behind us. It
was nice to know that they were there for our first time exploring
another new territory. One big pine tree had large branches with
some of them low enough to make it easy to climb. So I went up to
the first branch that was large enough to make a nice walkway.
When I turned around, I saw Sheba on a low, big branch. How did
she do that? Then I remembered the way she had climbed that wall
at the condo. The branch would be a safe place, to lie down, or for
just looking around.

From the tree we could see some more large trees laying down,
which also looked like neat places to hide, play, and climb. The
paths into the brush that led to the fallen trees had a faint scent of
other cats. Not seeing any, we climbed the trees to the highest
point. From there we could view the entire house, with it's back and
front yards. The sun felt good shining through the leaves, so we laid
down on the fallen tree for a short nap.

Mommy and Daddy had gone back into the house, but I felt they were keeping an eye on us. I must have been right, because as soon as we awoke they both came back out. All of us really had fun exploring the lot. At the edge of the trees was another empty lot with a house on the other side of it. As I stepped out of the wooded area, Daddy told me <u>no</u>! After a few steps, I knew why. I could smell that a dog had been there.

Sheba and I liked our new place. We were able to go in and out by ourselves and we had so many places to sleep, and explore. It was just like old times.

When we were settled into our new and real home, all of our routines had returned to the way they were at our old home. I again met Daddy each afternoon and he and I again worked in the yard, just like old times. However, Sheba had to be carried in order for her to be able to go outside. Her arthritis was so bad she could no longer do very much without help. She spent more and more time just sleeping.

One day, Mommy and Daddy put Sheba in her carrier and took her to the doctors. When they returned, Sheba was not with them. They told me that very bad arthritis had destroyed the joints in her legs. They explained that Sheba wouldn't be coming home anymore, but that she was no longer suffering.

After a few days, I understood what they were telling me. This time the doctor wasn't able to make her well. After I realized that she was not coming back, I saw her in a dream. Sheba explained that she was in heaven with no more pain and everything was peaceful. "Cats do go to heaven," she had told me, "and I'll see *you* there." That dream made me feel better, although I still missed her company for quite some time.

To help me get over the emptiness I felt, Mommy and Daddy spent a lot more time with me. I'm sure it helped them accept the loss of Sheba also. Daddy busied himself outside, planting new shrubs for me to hide behind. I really enjoyed helping him just like old times, and it also helped me adjust to life without Sheba.

One day when Daddy went inside after working in the yard, he left a bench just below the side window. When Mommy saw me on the pile of fallen trees next door, she opened the window to speak to me. Seeing and hearing her, I ran over below the window. She opened the window all the way and saw me sitting on the bench. She thought this was cute. "Smokie was sitting on the bench like a little old man," she said. "Come on inside." Then I really surprised her as I leaped through the window onto the seat inside.

I had just found a new way to get back into the house. From then on whenever I was outside sitting below the window on the bench, Mommy would open the window for me to jump inside. I got lots of praise for that new trick, and I had also trained them to allow me to use a short cut into the house.

Daddy brought a cardboard box home and renewed another fun game we used to play at our old home. I would jump in and out of it as he would scratch on the opposite side. The scratching sounded like a mouse and I would chase this imaginary mouse or play with my feathers and toys. Sometimes we used a paper bag from the grocery store. I loved playing in the boxes or bags, which had become real quality time for Daddy and me.

With Sheba gone, I slept more often with my Daddy. I slept next to his head with a paw around his neck. Sometimes it would get too hot and I would move to a window seat in the bedroom, where I could feel cool, fresh air, from an opened window. Daddy even spent more time outside with me, climbing on the fallen trees for a game of hide and seek. After the game, we would sit on the highest part of the tree where he would talk to me, as I looked at him affectionately.

I was getting older, as cats go, and should have been taking it easier. But it was just natural for me to jump, climb, and run just as fast as I did when I was younger. It was also my job to continue to protect Daddy's and my territory from other cats. I had been successful at chasing stray cats away that had returned to the fallen trees. However, it was time to take it easier, because I wanted to grow old with my Daddy, just like he had said to me so many times after Sheba was gone. It was during these times that he would call me his little Guardian Angel. Without knowing it, I really was going to help Daddy in another way.

So it was, that one day after he left for work in the morning, I had a bad seizure that made me fall off the window seat, where I was watching the water. After I hit the floor, I felt really terrible. I just wanted to be alone and wait for Daddy to come home. So I went upstairs, and as I climbed into a chair, I found that if I laid real still, the bad feeling got better and I was able to go to sleep while waiting for Daddy.

I don't know how long I slept, but I heard Daddy come home. Mommy told him that I had been upstairs all day. When Daddy came up to the bedroom, I was so glad to see him that I let out a big mroow. He picked me up gently and started carrying me downstairs. Halfway down the stairs, I began frothing at the mouth and had trouble breathing. Mommy ran to the phone, called the doctor and then she and Daddy rushed me to the office.

The doctor carried me to the back room and placed me and my blanket on the floor of a big cage. She left the door open so Mommy and Daddy could comfort me. The doctor put an intravenous feed tube in my leg and gave me some medicine that calmed me. Then she took some pictures of my insides to see what was wrong. When the pictures were developed the doctor showed them to Mommy and Daddy. I could tell that something was very bad. The pictures showed that all of my inside parts had been pushed against my chest and there wasn't any way to help me. Daddy came over to me and looked at me tearfully. I could see he was very upset. It was then I let him sense I understood and that it was okay. I tried to think about Sheba's message to me about going to Heaven, but because he was so upset he couldn't understand what I meant. He did know that prolonging what had to be done would only mean more suffering for me. I again sent him a message that I understood and that it was going to be all right.

I knew he had made the right decision, and looked at him with loving understanding and trust. Daddy looked at Mommy and she agreed, but was so upset she had to leave in tears. He signed some papers giving the doctor permission to put me to sleep and end my suffering. Daddy came over and thought about how much he loved me. He stayed for a few minutes until he saw that I was very peaceful.

As I went into a comfortable sleep Daddy also left in tears. It was then that I became aware of how I was to help my Daddy. I really would be his Guardian Angel. His memories of our love didn't die, and I helped him accept my death just like he had helped me when Sheba died. Although Daddy wasn't always aware that it was me, I helped him remember things we had done together that were good times. With my help, he was to be able to talk about me without feeling quite so sad.

Then the day came when I knew he was ready to understand what I had tried to let him know in the doctor's office. I remembered that Sheba had come to me in a dream and now I could go to him in a dream. A dream would allow me to have all the time I needed to explain this to Daddy and to ask him to put our fond memories in a book, so that other cat lover's could read about the love we had for each other.

Through a dream I let him know that cats, in this case me, were allowed in Heaven. I told him that Sheba and I were feeling fine and we would be waiting to see him again. Yes, Daddy finally knew that I really would be *Smokie Forever.*

P.S. Daddy didn't think he would ever love another cat—until he found "Itty Bitty".

0-595-29340-9